A Very Unusual Mary

An Anthology of Christmas Stories and Poems

Towcester U3A Creative Writing Group

Published by Towcester U3A Creative Writing Group
Publishing partner: Paragon Publishing, Rothersthorpe

First published 2021

© Towcester U3A Creative Writing Group, 2021

Illustrations by Richard Griffiths
© Richard Griffiths

Edited by James Brown

ISBN 978-1-78222-897-4

Book design, layout and production management by Into Print
www.intoprint.net
+44 (0)1604 832149

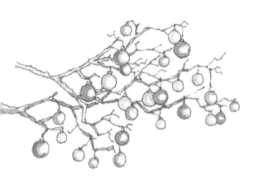

Written by

Kate Bartlett, Pippa Deycon, Peter Crickmore, Jeanette Ellwood, Barry
Hudley, Geoffrey Iley, Jane Morgan, Ann Ward and Anne Webb:
collectively, the writers of **Towcester U3A Creative Writing Group**
Edited by James Brown

Acknowledgments

The authors of these stories and poems came together through Towcester U3A's Creative Writing group. They are very grateful to Richard Griffiths whose wonderful illustrations have brought the stories and poems to life. You went above and beyond; to James Brown, whose wise editing have made our stories easier to read, and whose attention to detail was startling; and to Christine Russell for having beady eyes for grammatical mistakes and a forensic ability to see the finer detail.

Anne Webb would also like to express her thanks to Paula Smith and Ravensburger Ltd for their kind permission in allowing the BRIO name to be used in her story 'Jack's Letter'.

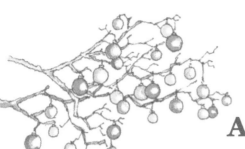

A Very Unusual Mary

CONTENTS

A village somewhere near you

JACK'S LETTER

by Anne Webb

St Ann's Children's Home, Oxford was not in Oxford at all, as Jack discovered, but in a small village just outside, called Marksoham. He knew his address off by heart when he had moved there 8 months ago.

As Jack was shown in for the first time he spotted 10 daffodil buds in a vase on the large hall table, in the large entrance hall. Jack was certain there were 10 as he had counted the yellow-green spears over and over again, trying so hard to keep his anxiety away; anything was useful to make him feel less nervous about this new start in his life, however mindless.

A notice hanging on the wall above the table announced

"WELCOME TO OUR HOME"

As Matron bustled in from an office, she held out her hand.

"Welcome to our home!" she said, proudly, "come with me and I'll show you to your new bedroom and introduce you to your new friends."

Jack looked back at the daffodils and thought they reminded him of a jar of artists brushes that had been dipped in yellow paint then put in the jar, upside down. He wanted to tell Matron about the daffodils and what they looked like but he wasn't sure she'd be interested.

Jack remembered that day, all those months ago, now that there were no daffodils in the hall or anywhere for that matter. Instead, the vase had twigs, sprayed silver. Small red shiny baubles hung from white ribbons.

Jack roomed with Chris. Chris was short for Christian not Christopher. This was obviously important to Chris as he told anyone that was new.

"I'm Chris! That's short for Christian not Christopher," Chris had explained to Jack on their first meeting.

Chris, 'short-for-Christian-not-Christopher' was 8 years old and 3 years older than Jack. Jack looked up to him like a big brother. The other 'roomy' was Yannis. It was pronounced 'Janny' but spelt Y-A-N-N-I-S.

"That's Y-A-N-N-I-S but you don't say the S" as Yannis would tell anyone that was new. Yannis was 6. So, Jack thought of him a bit more like a friend.

Jack was simply Jack, not short for Jackson or anything, so Jack would tell anyone that was new it was

"Jack, J-A-C-K but you don't pronounce the K" [but he secretly knew that you did].

Chris, short-for-Christian-not-Christopher had helped when Jack and Yannis ["don't-say-the-S] had to write their letters to Father Christmas. Chris "short-for-Christian-not-Christopher" knew how to set it out with their address at the top right hand corner and to start it off with Dear and finish it off with Yours sincerely.

Jack had only wanted a teddy-bear but Chris 'short-for-Christian-not-Christopher' said he couldn't ask for something like that. Chris "short-for-Christian-not-Christopher" had told him that he was too old for a teddy.

He said Jack had to ask Father Christmas for a new engine for his BRIO train set. Chris "short-for-Christian-not-Christopher" *also* had a BRIO train set and Jack wondered if that was the **real** reason that he wanted Jack to ask for that.

Jack wrote ...

Room 17
St Ann's
21 -23 King Street
Marksoham
Oxford
OX 5 8BB
2nd December

Dear Father Christmas,
Please may I have a new engine for my BRIO train set.
Thank you.
Yours sincerely
Jack

"Will he know who Jack is?" Jack asked Chris "short-for-Christian-not-Christopher". "Should I write my second name?"

"No" said Chris, who had signed *his* letter as Chris "short-for-Christian-not-Christopher".

Jack wondered if Father Christmas ever called himself "Father-Chris-short-for-Christmas"?

Jack knew that Yannis had wanted a Pirate Ship but Jack noticed that he too had asked for an engine for a BRIO Train set... and Yannis didn't even *have* a BRIO train set!

All Jack had really ever wanted was a teddy. He pictured the teddy that Father Christmas was now no longer going to bring him. It would have had a black nose, stitched with black wool that would feel slightly fluffy. Its eyes would be warm, dark brown, shiny bright ones that Jack could see his reflection in. Its light brown fluffy tummy would be fat and stuffed full so that Jack could push it in, in fun, and it would pop right out again. The arms and legs would be particularly soft and floppy and fluffy so Jack could pretend they were wrapped around him.

He would have been a cuddle-bear and a best friend.

It was midnight on Christmas eve and Father Christmas had almost finished for the night.

The St Ann's Children's Home, Oxford was almost the last home on his list. It was a rather bigger home than the normal sized home on his list.

"Rather more children than your normal sized house" thought Father Christmas. *"Rather more presents to deliver here!"*

The snow was too deep for the reindeer to go any closer and anyway, the reindeer's bells could sometimes wake up light sleepers. So Father Christmas took the presents that he needed out of his sack and piled them up into an impossibly high, teetering tower of toys. It seemed to anyone looking, like it was going to topple at any minute. But this was Father Christmas and things didn't always happen to him in the way that they might happen to other people.

At the very top-most of the pile was a teddy bear who had a black nose, stitched with black wool that felt slightly fluffy, whose eyes were warm, dark brown and shiny bright. Its light brown fluffy tummy was fat and stuffed full. The teddy's arms and legs were particularly soft and floppy and fluffy. He was a proper cuddle-bear.

Father Christmas made his slow climb towards the large house of St Ann's Children's Home and with each large stride the tower of toys shook and teetered even more, making them *even* **more** unstable.

Father Christmas didn't notice that the very top-most toy fell off. … Father Christmas didn't feel the change in the weight of his tower of toys and Father Christmas didn't hear the very top-most toy fall because the snow was so thick that it cushioned the toy's fall and muffled the noise. Father Christmas didn't notice that the teddy bear was no longer on his tower of toys…

When Father Christmas walked in to the last room, number 17, he first went to Chris' bed.

"Here you are Chris-short-for-Christian … and not Christmas" he whispered and chuckled silently to himself and placed a BRIO engine for a BRIO train set into the awaiting stocking.

He walked over to Yannis' bed and put a Pirate Ship into the expectant stocking.

Soon, all the toys had been safely stored in their rightful stockings, all except one. At Jack's bed, Father Christmas realised with shock that he no longer had a teddy bear for Jack. He looked around with growing anxiety. NO, no teddy bear to be seen. He remembered that the teddy bear had been the very top-most toy.

Horrified, Father Christmas realised that the teddy bear must have fallen off the impossibly tall tower of toys. In a panic, he reached into his big deep pocket and pulled out a brand new BRIO engine, for a BRIO train set. The box was a bit battered but it was all he had. He put it quickly into Jack's stocking and left.

By April the snow was just a distant memory and the daffodils had replaced the sparkling white with their custard yellow blooms once again.

Jack was helping the gardener pick the weeds that were already starting to shoot. There, under a big pine tree, in amongst the fallen dark brown pine needles and piles of dark brown pine cones was also something else brown but lighter in colour. An arm was just poking out from the tree litter as if it was waving. Jack pulled at the arm. He pulled until all the teddy bear came free. It wasn't a bear with a black nose, stitched with black wool that felt slightly fluffy. It was a nose that was grey and the wool felt matted. Its eyes were a warm, dark brown but no longer shiny bright. Its faded light brown fluffy tummy wasn't fat nor stuffed full so that when Jack pushed it in it didn't pop out again. The arms and legs were no longer soft and floppy and fluffy they were a bit hard in places. But Jack knew this was *his* cuddle-bear.

Jack wrapped his arms around him and gave him the biggest hug you can imagine.

"Hello Tom short-for-Tomaz" he said.

"Welcome to my home."

14

RED DOOR, WHITE WALL AND SHINY FLOOR FIND A HOME

By Ann Ward

"**Hullooooooa!**" said White Wall. "What have we *here*? I've been wondering when he would give me a door."

"Oh, hi there" said Red Door. "My paint has only just dried out. This place looks very shiny and new. How long have you been here?"

"Oh, not long" said Wall. "He finished painting me last weekend."

"Where *are* we?" asked Door.

"We're in a workshop of some kind. Look, when he opens that big door you can see outside. I must say, I hope you don't get any big ideas painted that ridiculous pillar box red. Why on earth did he choose that colour! Are *all* you doors painted like that?"

15

"Where are we?" asked Door

Door was a bit taken aback. "Well, I think it's a *lovely* colour. And it was left over from some decorating he did somewhere or other. Anyway," he said triumphantly "I bet you don't know what's on your other side."

"That's true" said Wall. "But of course, I'm *much* more important than you. You just fill a space, I hold the roof up! The place would collapse without me."

"I think you've both forgotten someone" growled a deep voice. "I am your very foundation. Without me you would both simply not be able to stand. I go everywhere and know what's going on behind simple walls and doors like you."

Shiny Floor did have a point there.

"Well, let's not argue" Door pleaded. "We do seem to be all complete now. Do you think we'll be here for ever? Why has he spent all this time putting us together?"

"I think there's something special going on very soon. I've been here long enough to see all sorts of comings and goings. They've been putting some beautiful lights up in the fir trees and every time he arrives home he has lots of parcels. We'll see soon enough no doubt."

Time passed... night fell, lights switched off, all was dark and quiet.

"Hey, you two" whispered Wall. "I hear footsteps. Something's happening."

The big door swung open and two dark figures came towards White Wall, Red Door and Shiny Floor. They felt themselves raised and carried clumsily outside under the starlit sky.

Door grew very excited – due to being bright red of course – while Wall was quite calm and collected and Floor was enjoying the rocking motion and the starlight reflected in his shiny surface. They felt themselves set down and then lots of other objects were squeezed around them. They were aware of still, cold fresh air, human voices, animal noises, bells jingling, a whip cracking ... and then White Wall felt such a rush of wind he thought he would be blown away.

Then came shouts and cries, whoops and laughter and a big voice boomed out

"We're off, hold tight Elves. We've got LOTS of children to deliver to tonight!"

"I think there's something special going on..."

ELVIS AND ELVIRA

By Jane Morgan

"Who are they?" I hear you ask.

Well, they are the littlest – and the naughtiest – of Santa's elves. A few years ago, playing hide-and-seek, Elvis had nearly been given away because he'd hidden in a box, been wrapped up and put on the sleigh before the other packing elves saw the 'present', in other words Elvis, wriggling about. My goodness, the Chief Elf had been cross, but, had they learned their lesson? No, they had not. Last year, they'd been caught decorating the reindeer's antlers with tinsel and trimmings. Rudolph and his team were NOT pleased; they'd huffled and puffled and grunted and snorted and had to be given extra carrots to calm down.

These two little elves are, of course, still Santa's Helpers, but they're quite low grade. Every year, two Sleigh Elves are chosen to ride with Santa to give him the right present for each house, and, they've *never* even made the short list.

At the moment, everyone's working really hard, because it's the Night Before You Know What, so it's packing and labelling time. There are some really good presents; Elvis wouldn't mind having the massive jigsaw and Elvira would love that big train set, but they know they're for good boys and girls.

Oh, sorry, did I say, "*Everyone's* working really hard?" Hmm, well, that's all the elves, apart from Elvis and Elvira. They were on labelling duty, but they got bored and started to stick labels on all sorts of places you shouldn't: they stuck them on the sides of the present not the middle; then on the back; then upside down; then, getting sillier, on each other's pointy ears, on each other's noses and, you've guessed it, yes, on each other's bottoms.

It was *really* good fun. Until...

"What's all this giggling? What are you two up to now?" said a cross voice. Oh dear, it was the Chief Elf again; she had a very big nose and was looking over her glasses at them.

"Nothing," said Elvis quickly.

"He made me do it," said Elvira at *exactly* the same time.

"We just haven't got time for messing about," Chief Elf said sternly, "Santa's due to start the Australia section in forty minutes, so it's the *Naughty Shelf* for you both."

Elves, you see, are so small, they fit very nicely onto human-sized shelves and there really wasn't much room in the crowded, busy workshop tonight. As well as all the other elves on 'E' shift, there was a mountain of presents at one end; then Ermintrude and Egbert in the wrapping section; followed by Elton and Ethel on label printing and, lastly, a very important elf, Epicentre by name, was using a Santa Satnav to sort everything into huge piles according to regions for the sleigh delivery.

Elvis and Elvira looked at each other – The Naughty Shelf **again!** "Oh, but we wanted…"

"*No wanting about it*," said Chief Elf smartly (she did so enjoy her job), "Santa's worried about the weather; we need hard working elves, not mischief makers. Up on that shelf – *NOW!*"

I say, 'Naughty Shelf', but really it was a chilly, dusty windowsill, Elvira sneezed and Elvis, chin on hands, sighed. They'd blown it again – Sleigh Elf – huh, Shelf Elf was more like it. And now, they wouldn't have the Mince Pie and Milk treat that was meant to give everyone a last energy boost before packing up the sleigh, hitching up the reindeer and zooming off into the night sky.

Those pies did smell yummy and looked de-lic-ious, too, soft and sugary.

Elvira's mouth watered and Elvis sighed again – loudly this time just in case any of the other elves felt sorry for them and passed them up a spare mince pie... no such luck.

"OK, elves, break's over. Back to work," said Chief Elf briskly. She did seem to enjoy her job a bit *too* much.

Soon the workshop was filled again with the noise of sticky tape ripping, paper rustling, presents being passed to Eduardo and Effie, the bigger elves, who were loading up the sleigh, but – wait a minute – then there was another noise.

It went like this, "**Oᵒᵒн**" and this "**Urgн**" and then this,

"**Oᵒн**, my...stom-ach."

Elvira nudged Elvis who'd been idly picking his nose and eating it (Well, he was hungry; he hadn't had a mince pie, remember).

"Why have their faces gone green?" she said.

"Dunno...ooh, *look*, Ermintrude's bending over and clutching her tummy..."

"Epicentre's got his hand over his mouth."

My goodness, Santa had some very sick elves. No-one knew whether it was a dodgy mince pie or the funny-tasting milk, but here's a hint – never drink funny tasting milk, because those elves were *very* poorly.

Everyone rushed outside, so Elvis and Elvira rubbed the dirt off the window behind them and gazed out into the snow.

"*WOW*, look at *THAT*!" said Elvira as Egbert's sick shot through the air and covered Elton's pointy red shoe even though he was quite a distance away. Poor Elton looked at Egbert in horror, then down at his sick-covered shoe and was promptly sick again – all over the other one.

Then the door opened, there was a gust of powdery snow and they heard.

"HO, HO, HO!"

Well, you can guess who *that* was.

"Just practising my entrance in case any boys and girls wake up," said Santa to the Chief Elf, who was sitting on the floor in a heap of ribbons desperately trying not to vomit in front of him. "I've been setting the Santa Satnav. Any mince pies and milk left?" he asked rubbing his tummy, "I do hope I haven't missed the Pre-Sleigh Ride Treat."

"I'm afraid you have," said Elvira, who was always quick to update others.

"Who's that?" asked Santa looking around and, finding the workshop surprisingly empty, called "Elvis and Elvira? What are you doing up there? Come down *AT ONCE*."

"Well, the Chief Elf said..."

"Oh, never mind all that. Where are all the others? We must choose the Sleigh Elves and then get going. Those presents won't deliver themselves...My goodness," he said, looking through the open door, "what are they all doing out there, having a snowball fight?"

"Not exactly," said Elvira, "they all had the Mince Pie and Milk Treat..."

Santa looked worried, very worried indeed, "Oh, dear me, but tonight's the night...."

"...but **we** didn't have any mince pies and..." Elvis finished hopefully.

"You *mean*...?" Santa looked even more worried.

"There's only us, I'm afraid," Elvira said meekly, but in a tone that she hoped sounded like a very good, hard working, just-the-elf-you-need-in-a-crisis sort of voice.

There was a pause, a long pause; you could hear Ellipsis being very sick "**BLe-UgH**!" for a second time.

"Right," said Santa briskly – he'd had to cope with worse than this over the years – "coats, hats and gloves on you two. You're our Sleigh Elves this year."

"WHOOP, WHOOP!" said Elvis.

"Gloves! Do we have to?" Elvira cried.

"It's cold, up there, very, VERY cold," said Santa.

So, they muffled up, gave the reindeer an Extra Energy Carrot each, checked the Santa Satnav and they were off.

He was right: it was very cold; the sky was black and they were going so fast, the stars turned into ribbons of light.

"WOWZERS!" said Elvira; Elvis still had his hand over his eyes and was feeling a bit travel sick.

Once the reindeer had finished puffing and snorting and they'd got used to the cold air swooshing past them, everything was silent and very still as the sleigh travelled over the big, black oceans. *BUT*, when there were parcels to deliver they worked harder than they'd ever worked in their little elf-lives. Elvira was good at holding the sleigh steady and general reindeer-control when Santa was down chimneys, delivering parcels; while Elvis, being a good reader, was excellent at label and address reading. Although they did have to park on the roof of Wilhelmina Hinklebottom-Molotovski-Fanshawe's house for quite some time, while they worked out whether that was just one girl... or perhaps three?

It got even colder as they got nearer the North Pole, so they snuggled into Santa's nice cuddly red coat and dreamed of hot chocolate. As they landed, Ermintrude and Ellipsis were feeling much better and so helped with the reindeer: more carrots, hay and a good rest were needed.

Santa carried in two very sleepy elves and tucked a snuggly blanket around them in the armchair by the fire.

He put two carefully wrapped boxes with a Sleigh Elf medal in each on the table beside them and said, very quietly,

"Well done, little elves. Good night, sleep tight."

And they did.

SANTA'S DILEMMA

By Kate Bartlett

Santa was worried... *very* worried indeed.

It was two weeks before Christmas, the most important day of the year for him. The day he had to get everything right. All the children's letters from Britain had all been delivered in good time, so he knew exactly what he had to prepare to fill their stockings on Christmas Eve. This year it seemed an even bigger list than usual. But there was a huge problem; the elves in the British Division had flu – nearly all of them. They were going down like ninepins. And without his elves he had nobody to prepare the stocking presents. He had never let the children down before, and he was determined not to do so this year, but he had no idea at all what to do about it.

He sighed heavily, and went to see Sylvia, his Chief Elf for the British Grotto. He found her in the workshops, dashing back and forth, fetching wrapping paper and ribbon from one bench and toys from another, and wrapping as fast as she could. There were only ten other elves there. Normally Santa had over a hundred, all working flat out at this time of year. Sylvia's hair was almost standing on end as she raced up and down the workshop. The other elves, though, seemed to be going quite slowly and Santa was afraid that they were beginning to feel ill as well. He really could not afford to lose any more.

"I can't talk now, Santa." Sylvia hurtled past him on her way back to the present table. "We are really not going to make it this year. You are the boss. It's *your* responsibility. What is your plan?" She flew back in the other direction, an X-Box in one hand and a teddy bear in the other.

"Oh don't," groaned Santa. "I wish I *had* a plan, but I have no idea what to do."

"Well, it's not going to help you just standing there in my way." Sylvia pushed past him, trailing parcel ribbon. "Go and do your job! Work out how we are going to get all the presents out for Christmas Eve."

Santa wondered if there were any other elves at North Pole HQ who could help. He rang the Elf Agency in Greenland, but they just said everyone on their books was already hard at work at this time of year, and wasn't that obvious to him, given he was in charge of it all. That was rather rude, but Santa was too anxious to argue.

He wandered round the gardens in despair, chewing the straggling hair of his beard, not noticing it getting caught in his teeth. He barely saw the beautiful trees draped in tinsel, with their sparkling decorations and winking fairy lights – hang on a minute! *Fairy lights – FAIRIES...* Santa stopped dead in his tracks, chewing harder on his beard, which made the white hair sticking out each side of his mouth waggle up and down in excitement... Maybe there were some fairies who could help him!

"He barely saw the beautiful trees draped in tinsel…"

He rushed back to his grotto, grabbed the Elf phone, and typed "fairy availability" into the search engine. He got the number of the Queen of the Fairies and went to FaceTime. Amazingly, she appeared immediately, straightening her diamond tiara and waving a wand imperiously.

"Well, I knew it was you calling," she said. "I *am* magic, you know. I'm a fairy, in case you hadn't realised."

Santa was a bit taken aback. He had expected the Queen of the Fairies to be a bit more polite. Anyway, he explained his problem, and she paused a moment to think.

"*Hmmm*, now let me see...

No, I can't let you have any fairies at all. I need them for the tops of all those Christmas trees. And then there are *so* many pantomimes to provide GOOD Fairies for! I just haven't got one to spare. You are not the only one who has responsibilities at this time of year, you know. I can't help you at all, sorry. But you do realise, don't you, that it will be a *dreadful* disaster if the presents don't get out on time. You *are* aware of that, I hope! You are going to have to solve it. Think of all those disappointed children with nothing in their stockings – and their parents still trying to make Christmas Day fun! It doesn't bear thinking about!

Sorry, I have to go now and design the new wands for this year – so important to get the wand just right, don't you think? *Byeeee!*"

And she was gone. No help at all. What now? Santa stuffed a bit of beard back in his mouth and decided to go and check on the reindeer. At least they were all healthy and ready to go.

They were so pleased to see him! Rudolf stamped his feet happily and almost broke out of his stall. Prancer and Dancer made loud, excited honking noises and waved their antlers wildly.

"It's *so* good to see you, Santa. You haven't been to see us for *ages*! We hear the elves are poorly. Do give them our love. We miss them. They are such fun! Oh, Santa, what's the matter? You look so sad?"

"Well, I really don't think we are going to have the British stocking presents ready in time for Christmas Eve with all the elves ill this year, and that's terrible! I just don't know what to do. We need at least an extra two weeks to get things ready with so few elves able to work."

Rudolph pricked up his ears. "Two weeks," he said, thinking hard and frowning with concentration. *(Have you ever seen a reindeer frown? Not a pretty sight!)* "Well, you know I went on holiday to Germany this year? I had a great time with the German reindeer and the elves in your German division, Santa. We got very friendly. Do you know, in Germany they do things differently from in Britain? They open their stockings *(well, actually, they use shoes instead, but that's a detail)* on December 6th. That's when Saint Nicholas gave out sweets and things to the children whose families were so poor, they couldn't afford presents. And that's why we have stockings, too! Oh! But you ARE Saint Nicholas, aren't you! Of course you are, so you should know this already!

"I do indeed. But what's your point?" asked Santa, puzzled.

"My point is that... it was December 6th on Monday, so the German elf teams have finished their biggest orders! They won't be doing very much at the moment! They might be able to help."

"Rudolf, you're **BRILLIANT!**" exclaimed Santa as he turned on his heels and ran back to the grotto.

Within half an hour, he had made arrangements with the Chief Elf at his German grotto and a contingent of German elves were on their way. Christmas was *SAVED!* All the stocking presents would get out on time, and it would be ***THE BEST CHRISTMAS EVER!***

Santa rewarded Rudolf for saving the situation – he allowed him to decorate his nose with tinsel and it glowed with pride because it was his idea that saved Christmas!

Thank goodness we don't all do things in exactly the same way!

"I've got an angel comin' to tea"

A VERY UNUSUAL MARY

By Jeanette Ellwood

'I want to be different,' thought Jennie 'then maybe people will love me even though I'm the new girl. They don't love me now.

'I don't know what to do, I don't think I'm nice to look at or even clever.'

Her tears fell as she pondered,

'I'm going to be Mary in our Christmas play tomorrow. I wonder if I could wear my best dress, at least I'd look pretty then.'

The small figure poised centre stage, bright yellow duster in one hand, brush in the other. It rose on tiptoes and twirled, revealing all the glory of a pink, spangled tutu and grubby ballet shoes.

Audience eyes goggled.

"I'm Mary," Jennie announced, moving to the table in the middle of the stage and giving it a swipe with the duster. "I'm doing housework 'cos I've got an angel comin' to tea with news of great happiness – which is why I've got my spangly dress on.

"*AND...*" she confided, "I'm pregnant, God is the father, my baby's name is Jesus and I'm going riding on a donkey with my, *erm...*" she faltered, looking round towards stage left... *"Erm..."*

"Fiancé" hissed a voice. *"Fiancé."*

"Yes," said Mary, "that's right, my fiancé," she took a breath. "Lots of angels are going to sing and we're going to get lots of presents for our new baby."

After making sure she had everyone's full attention she rose on tiptoe and gave another twirl.

A boy dressed in a Dunelm dressing gown peered round the potted plant which was standing in for an olive tree stage left.

"Hello," he said to no one in particular, "I'm Joseph."

He glanced at Mary,

"Are you ready? Where's your suitcase? We're going to Bethlehem you know. It's a long way."

He looked disparagingly at the tutu,

"That dress is no good, you can't go in that, you'll need a coat."

Mary produced her doll's suitcase, opened it and took out a pink chiffon scarf which she draped round her shoulders.

"I'm ready now," she replied brightly.

Joseph opened his mouth to comment on the scarf, saw Mary's glare and shut it again.

"Hello ... I'm Joseph"

"Told you that scarf was all wrong, it's not warm enough and should be blue."

He muttered audibly to himself. "Mary *always* wears blue, on all our Christmas cards she's wearing blue."

"That's my best silk scarf for heaven's sake," her mother whispered indignantly to her friend in the audience. "She didn't ask me, the naughty girl."

Jennie turned to give her a brilliant, slightly guilty smile as she linked arms with a plainly reluctant Joseph and almost dragged him off stage as the curtains slowly and jerkily closed.

A small hand poked through a gap in the curtains and pointed to the group of children getting raggedly to their feet at the front of the stage.

A muffled voice hissed

"By the way, these are the singin' angels. *Go on Miss, QUICK, it's time...*"

The hand disappeared and the piano hastily started to play *Away in a Manger* and everyone began to sing those well loved words.

Behind the closed curtains Mary and Joseph settled themselves on low stools in the middle of the stage. Around them were nursery school toddlers encased in creamy wool sheep-suits, with a couple of shepherds and three kings waiting in the wings ready to carry their very special presents of a gold cardboard box, a bottle of oil – for myrrh – and a bag of white bath salts – for frankincense.

In front of Mary was a wooden doll's cot filled with hay and sitting in the middle of that was a baby-sized doll, dressed in bright sparkly clothes, chosen by Jennie.

As the curtains opened, the ox and ass crept their way into the tableau amidst *oohs* and *aahs* as everyone admired the scene while craning their necks to look for their very own child.

The choir began to sing *We Three Kings*... when one of the lambs scrambled to its feet crying.

"I don't like this, it's too scratchy, I want it off! I want it off!" she said as she tried to scramble out of the woolly suit, tears running down her cheeks. She fumbled frantically with the Velcro fastening as Mary with great presence of mind reached forward, tugged open the lamb-suit and lifted the little one clean out of it and plonked her on her knee.

"Don't cry darlin'," she said. "Here, hold the baby."

Joseph picked up the sparkly doll from the crib as Mary covered the lamb's vest and navy knickers by wrapping her in the precious scarf.

Tears forgotten, the happy toddler sat there, beaming at Mary and Joseph hugging that baby for all it was worth.

"Oh," sighed the audience in unison, *"what a lovely thing to do."*

The lamb's mother stood up and waved to her little one, calling out loudly,

"Thank you Jennie, that was *sooo* kind. She hates wool, it gives her a rash."

Mary smiled as she cuddled little-girl-lamb to keep her warm as she was starting to shiver, without her lamb outfit.

"She is such a sweetie," she said, "even though she's not a lamb any more."

Everyone clapped and smiled back.

"You are such a kind girl. ***WE ALL LOVE YOU LOTS.***"

THE HOOLIGOATS AND LONELY MR GOHTURD

By Barry Hudley

One evening, in the middle of December not too many years ago, the four Hooligoats lay in their dark shed in Pets Corner, and snuggled up in their soft, warm, hay. Outside, it was a cloudless night, the moon shone brightly and the stars seemed to be dancing because they twinkled so much in the sky. Frost was settling on the grass and on the trampoline in their play-park, and it was so cold that ice was already beginning to form on the four containers of fresh drinking water that had been left for them. Three of the pygmy goats, Barney, Cuthbert and Fernando, were busily chewing strands of hay. Ralph, however, was deep in thought.

After a while, Barney stopped eating.

'Ralph,' he said. 'You're very quiet. What are you plotting now?'

Now, you may have heard rumours that the Hooligoats are always plotting something reckless or dastardly. On this occasion, however, Ralph had an odd, fuzzy, Christmassy feeling.

'I was actually thinking about Christmas Dinner,' he replied.

'Huh,' Cuthbert jeered, 'you're *always* thinking of your stomachs.'

'Well,' insisted Ralph, 'I have got four of them, so that seems fair enough to me.'

'Shertainly doesh,' said Barney, who'd started eating again and had a fresh mouthful of hay. 'Now let the goat shpeak, Cussbert.'

'Anyway,' continued Ralph, 'I was thinking about Christmas Dinner because of a conversation that I overheard between bossy Mrs Bradbury, who owns Pets Corner, and our lovely Mr Gohturd.'

The sound of sniggering came from the darkness. Ralph sighed.

'What's so funny, Fernie? Was it because I said the name *Gohturd*?'

Fernando stifled another giggle. 'Sorry,' he said, 'sorry, sorry. *Not* funny.' And promptly sniggered again.

'Fernie, do *shut up*!' Barney said firmly. 'What did they shay, Ralph?'

Ralph continued. 'Well, apparently, his wife died ten years ago, and he'll be all by himself again for Christmas. He's been so very good looking after us, I was thinking we should invite him round for Christmas Dinner. Put on a spread, kind of thing.'

'We can't do that, Ralph,' said Barney, alarmed, 'he'd be expecting roast turkey, and you know that eating other animals is unthinkable.'

"What's so funny, Fernie?"

'*Ah*, but he wouldn't expect meat at all, Barney,' explained Ralph. 'Bossy Bradbury said that she couldn't possibly invite him round to hers because he's a *vegan*, which means he doesn't eat animals. We could buy some nice vegan food from the Pets Corner Café. I'm sure Bronwen wouldn't mind us having some.'

'We don't have any money left, Ralph,' Cuthbert observed. 'So did you *actually* mean to say that we could go through the secret door in the café and, sort of, *borrow* some nice vegan food?'

'Er, yes,' admitted Ralph.

'Count me in,' chorused the others joyfully.

So it was, just three days before Christmas, that Barney, Cuthbert, Fernando and Ralph went round the other animals in Pets Corner to make sure they were all invited to the party. As they were talking to the family of meerkats, Barney suddenly gasped, and nudged Ralph to get his attention.

'Shouldn't we invite Mr Gohturd as well?' he asked.

Fernando started sniggering again.

'I wish we could,' replied Ralph, trying hard to ignore Fernie, 'but people are generally not smart enough to understand Hoolispeak, even though we can understand everything that people say. Still, never fear, I've worked out a way to get him here on Christmas day. All we need to do now is to, erm, *borrow* the party food.'

That very night, a number of items of food mysteriously disappeared from the café, together with two dozen party hats and crackers that had been reserved for the family-get-together of Bossy Bradbury. Unfortunately, next day and unbeknown to the lads, Bronwen Beyer, who did all of the cooking in the café, noticed that some of her tastiest offerings had vanished overnight, and vowed to find out who had taken it. Would she discover that the Hooligoats were the culprits?

Well, on the morning of Christmas Eve, Bronwen did what she often did. She went round to see the Hooligoats, and to feed them some linseed chips, which she knew was their favourite of all treats. She was about to buy some from the gumball machine that was next to their shed when she realised it was empty.

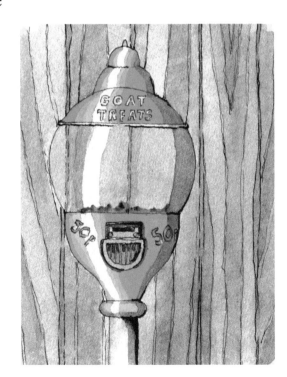

'Odd,' said Bronwen as she shook the gumball machine, 'it's *empty*. Still, not to worry, I'll get some from the sack in the shed.'

The Hooligoats panicked.

'*SHE'S GOING INTO OUR SHED*,' Ralph hissed to the others. 'She'll find our party food.'

They all held their breath and waited.

Bronwen opened the shed door, and was about to go inside when she suddenly stopped.

'The stolen food,' she said aghast, 'it's all in here. *You…you…*' She turned and pointed an accusing finger at Ralph, 'You little *TEA-LEAF*, you. I can't believe you took all this food. I'll have to tell Mrs Bradbury. She'll be really *CROSS*.'

Ralph bleated apologetically.

Fortunately, Bronwen was smarter than the average human. 'Sorry, eh? Just borrowing it eh? I'll bet you're going to have a party?'

Ralph bleated again.

Bronwen nodded. 'I see. A Christmas party for Mr Gohturd eh? I really like Mr Gohturd, he's such a nice man and he shouldn't be lonely at Christmas.'

Another bleat from Ralph.

Bronwen thought for a moment, then nodded again. 'Okay, but I was also going to be by myself tomorrow, so I'll overlook it if I can come along as well.' She looked again at the food in the shed. 'I see you haven't got any vegetable sausages. I do like my vegetable sausages. I'll bring some with me when I come along for dinner tomorrow.' With that, she turned and went back to the café, completely forgetting about the linseed chips.

'Er, what happened there?' asked Fernando in amazement. 'Did Bronwen actually *understand* what you were bleating?'

'*Mmm*, it appears so,' replied Ralph, thoughtfully. 'And just as worrying, we seem to have another guest for Christmas Dinner.'

'Don't worry,' laughed Cuthbert. 'We just need to borrow a bigger nut-roast.'

Late the following morning, as the church bells were ringing out for Christmas Day, Ralph set off to get lonely Mr Gohturd, who lived high up on the hill in the next village. He'd thought that, if he just turned up outside his cottage and bleated loudly, Mr Gohturd would hear him and would be sure to take him back to Pets Corner.

He hadn't got very far along the lane, however, when a dirty truck drove past him at high speed, choking him with horrible exhaust fumes. He stood coughing for a while and then, when the smoke had cleared, he could see that the truck had stopped just a short way up the lane. He waited to see if anyone got out of the truck but no-one did, so he cautiously made his way until he was alongside the muddy back wheels. He was about to start running, when the door opened and a large, scruffy man got out.

It was Ernie Bogrott, a local farmer.

'Ere, strange likkle goatie wiv the big belly. Wot yer doin, all by yer lonesome? I bet I could take you 'ome, it'd be nice to 'ave a change from goose for Chrissmusdinna. There's a nice bitta meat on yer, ain't there? Probably 'nuff forra curry on Boxin' Day as well.'

He grabbed Ralph and bundled him into the open back of the truck, where he trussed his hooves together with some rope. Ralph cried out, bleating as loudly as he could, but Bogrott shouted back even louder at him. 'YER A NOISY LIKKLE DIVIL, BUT YEW WON'T BE SO ROWDY WHEN OI SLIT YER FROAT AN STICK YER IN THE COOKIN POT.' He jumped back into the cab, and drove off, with Ralph still crying out in the back.

Just at that time, Mr Gohturd had decided to go for a mid-day walk before tucking into his Christmas beans-on-toast. As he turned the corner by the village shop, he heard the roar of a truck coming up the lane. It stopped by the shop, and Ernie Bogrott got out to put some letters into the post-box. Mr Gohturd could hear a lot of bleating, and leaned over the side of the truck to see what was making so much noise.

'ERE, WOTCHER STARIN' AT?' shouted Bogrott, trying to push Mr Gohturd away.

'Th...that,' spluttered Mr Gohturd, 'that's Ralph, from Pets Corner. You've got my Ralphy.'

'Nah, yer mistaken, mate, thass my Chrissmusdinna, tha'ris. My missus'll love cookin 'im.'

'That's *MY* Ralphy and no-one, but *NO-ONE*, is cooking my Ralphy.'

Mr Gohturd swung his arm out and his elbow landed with a kerunch on Bogrott's nose. Bogrott fell to the floor, roaring in pain. Ralph bleated again, and felt himself being lifted from the truck. 'Now, let's get you untied,' said Mr Gohturd soothingly, 'and back to Pets Corner where you belong.' Off he strode, leaving Ernie sitting in the road, mopping his nose with his sleeve.

Mr Gohturd, with Ralph in his arms, opened the gate into Pets Corner and made his way to the field where the Hooligoats lived.

As he turned the corner by their shed, he stopped and stood, not quite believing what he saw. There in the field, seated at two long tables laden with food, were the other Hooligoats, most of the animals from Pets Corner, and Bronwen. Mr Gohturd really liked Bronwen, of course, but had been too shy to say anything to her.

Bronwen stood up and raised her glass in the air.

'Ralph has brought Mr Gohturd along. **HURRAH** and **HAPPY CHRISTMAS TO YOU**, Mr Gohturd,' she shouted, and all the animals cried out in agreement.

Mr Gohturd looked at Ralph, who nuzzled gently into his shoulder.

'Thank you, little friend,' Mr Gohturd whispered.

'No,' bleated Ralph quietly, 'thank *YOU*.'

You can read more adventures about the Hooligoats in *The Kat and The Hooligoats* and *Suet Begins*.
Details on *barryhudleyauthor@co.uk*."

"...the phantom legions come"

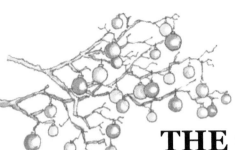

THE CHRISTMAS LEGIONS

A Victorian Pastiche by Geoffrey Illey

This is a Towcester legend, and it's one that's often told
    As Christmas Day approaches and the nights are bleak and cold.
Then Watling Street falls silent; gone is the traffic's hum.
And children hear a murmur, from the beat of a ghostly drum
As down the Roman highway the phantom legions come.
And as their ghostly sandals
March down the ancient street,
Their spirits sense those children
Who're tidy, clean and neat.
Then, Christmas Day will be a joy
For every virtuous girl and boy.

But as for those who've not been good – well, that's a different tale
They won't enjoy their Christmas; their toys will break and fail.
So, Towcester children, please be good, for if not you should fear
The march of phantom legions – and Christmastide is near!

"... change this junk into useful things"

CHRISTMAS SPELLS

By Pippa Deacon

The four children exchanged anxious looks and Jake, the eldest, whispered "What are we going to do now?" The four of them had been playing "*Harry Potter*" and the spell they had made up went wrong, horribly wrong. The youngest child, Bonnie, (from next door) had been turned into a gingery tabby cat.

Bonnie and her sister Ruby had come to play with Jake and Tom while their mother had gone to finish her Christmas shopping. They decided to make some magic, carefully choosing the right sort of spell, or so they thought, to change some old toys into some new ones, which they could give to the children in hospital as Christmas presents.

Carefully practising the words *"By the moon and the stars, the sun and the winds, change this junk into useful things"* and adding *"please"* as an afterthought. Bonnie had faded away and there in her place was this sweet little tabby cat, sitting amongst a tangle of half finished paper chains.

They, the three children and the cat, stared at each other and after a few moments, in what seemed like ages, the cat said

"What are you looking at? Haven't you seen a *cat* before?"

Tom collected himself and said

"Yes, of course we have, but not a *talking cat!* And where's Bonnie?"

"Ah," said the cat, "don't worry about her, she's fine. I understand you want to have some new toys, to give as presents, to unfortunate children who are in hospital over the holiday, is that right?"

The cat looked from one to the other and all the children nodded slowly, still rather shocked at this development.

Jake said looking at his watch, "It's nearly lunchtime, can we carry on this conversation after lunch?" Then he realised he would have to explain Bonnie's absence to Mum.

The cat once again said "Don't worry about that – all of you come closer and put your hands on my back."

The children moved closer and put their hands on the cat's back.

"Shut your eyes and leave the rest to me."

Almost at once they were aware of a soft whirring sound and they felt themselves being whizzed through the air… and then they landed with a soft bump.

When they opened their eyes, the scene that greeted them was a large warehouse, filled with every kind of gift they could imagine, with lots of small people picking things out and placing them them on waiting pallets. These, the tabby explained, were awaiting delivery on December the 24th.

One of the workers, a cheery roundish person in a green suit, greeted the cat with "Hello there Mustard! Who have we got here, eh?"

Mustard looked at his charges and answered "These three kind children need some presents for children in hospital, so perhaps you would give them a hand and show them where things are."

The little man, whose name was Thimble, said he would with pleasure, but they would have to be quick as the *"Boss"* needed him in ten minutes in the planning room.

Thimble bustled off, Mustard waved the children off with her paw,

"You'll be fine with Thimble, he'll look after you, take what you want."

The children trooped off to make their selections behind Thimble who was mumbling to himself. Jake thought he heard the little man saying something like *"It makes a change to have children thinking of others at this time of year"*. He led them to the star presents, reserved for very special children.

"Help yourselves" announced Thimble as he handed them each a sack in which to carry their choices.

Aware that time was short, the excited children made their selections, and Ruby even managed to get something small for Bonnie, hoping she would see her sister again!

When the sacks were full, Mustard appeared, and said

"Right oh! Children back home now I think, hold on and close your eyes."

Again the children touched her back, they heard the whirring sound, the rushing air, and felt a small soft bump, followed by another few bumps *[which was the sacks of toys]* and opened their eyes.

There on the chair, curled up in the muddle of paper chains... fast asleep, was Bonnie – but no sign of the little gingery cat.

From downstairs they heard Mum calling,

"COME ON YOU LOT, lunch is ready, wash your hands quickly as you can."

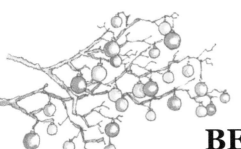

BELLS AT CHRISTMAS

A Victorian Pastiche by Geoffrey Illey

It was Christmas Eve in Towcester and all along Watling Street
Were throngs of happy revellers with Christmas fare replete.
But one poor shambling figure was not like all the rest,
A hunchbacked ragged pauper, his head sunk to his chest.
But suddenly he straightened up — and Quasimodo's hopes
Were buoyed by the sound of chiming bells as the ringers tugged their ropes.
He lumbered past the Market Square and then along Chantry Lane
Till he stood at the door of St. Lawrence Church and felt at home again.
True, it wasn't like Notre Dame, but this team clanged with the best;
Little they knew that the hunchback was about to make a request.
He beat his fists on the old oak door, *'OUVREZ LA PORTE!'*
he roared,

'I muss get up to ze bell tower for my strength to be restored.
If I miss my daily stint wiz ze bells, I'll wither and waste away —
So, permettez-moi to join you till ze break of Christmas Day.'

The bell-tower captain pondered, then yelled, 'Come in; feel free.'
Quasimodo sprang to a bell rope. *'Allez mes braves!'* cried he.

61

Then merry peals from Towcester rang through the Christmas night
And a flurry of gentle snowflakes created a landscape white.
And children as far as Abthorpe who heard those distant bells
Called out to their doting parents, 'We know what that sound foretells;
Those far-off bells are magical — they'll bring us such soothing rest,
We'll all have a wonderful Christmas and one that is truly blessed.'

Quasimodo enjoyed his Christmas with our bell-ringers of renown,
Wherever his travels take him, he'll remember our festive town.

"He stood at the door of St. Lawrence Church..."

"But Daddy, they're not kneeling"

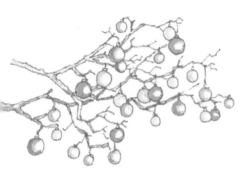

OXEN

By Peter Crickmore

"But Daddy, they're not kneeling," she wailed. Susan was good at wailing, because she had two older brothers who teased her a lot. Grown ups stared at her father briefly to see what he would do.

She and her Daddy were in their local church. It was Christmas Eve and they had come in out of the cold to see the annual display of the church's nativity scene under the stone pulpit.

The display was like a doll's house with one side removed. A thatched stable had a small light in the top, so, even in the church gloom, you could see the manger with Joseph and Mary standing behind it. Behind them were two oxen. Susan knew they were oxen not cows, because her Sunday School teacher had told her the story many times. They were very similar but oxen were for pulling carts and ploughing fields, cows were for milking.

"That's because..." said Daddy, wracking his brain for an explanation before Susan went into complete melt-down.

"That's because…" said the church Minister who had come up behind Susan and knew her well, "… that's because Baby Jesus is not there yet."

"Baby Jesus comes at midnight tonight," he went on. "Then the oxen will kneel down."

"Can I come back and see them kneel, Daddy *please*? *PLEASE?*" urged Susan, although she knew it was long past her bedtime.

"Well, perhaps you are old enough to stay up with your brothers this year," he promised.

Later that evening, widow Doris came in to the church to tidy up, as she had done for years since her husband died. When she came to the nativity scene she noticed that several of the figures had fallen over.

"That will never do," she said to herself as she reached over to stand Joseph and one of the angels upright. As she pulled her arm back, her sleeve caught the horns of the two oxen, knocking them over the edge onto the stone floor. Aghast, she found both the figures' front legs were broken off at the knees.

"The Minister won't like that," she muttered, wondering what to do. She tried sticking the broken legs back on with some Blue-Tack that was holding up a notice explaining the nativity scene to and where it was described in the Bible. It didn't work. Both oxen fell over as soon as she let them go.

Finally she had an idea. She pushed the broken pieces under the straw and stood the two oxen next to manger as if they were about to lie down – bending their knees first. Then she went to fetch the Minister and show him what had happened.

Far from telling her off, the Minister almost shouted:

"***Wonderful!*** We've never had them kneeling before! They're kneeling already!"

Not knowing quite what he was on about, Doris was nevertheless relieved, thinking, not for the first time, what a lovely man the Minister was.

That evening, true to his promise, Susan's father wrapped her in a duvet and drove with her two brothers back to church for the Midnight Service. The highlight for Susan, was when the Minister solemnly laid the Baby Jesus figure in the nativity scene and the choir sang the carol *Silent Night*.

"*SEE* Daddy," she said enthusiastically as they looked again at the figures on the way out, "the oxen are kneeling now!"

That was the first time she said it.

She said it again on the way home past the farm where the family bought their eggs and milk. All the cattle had moved into the open barn next to their house.

AND THEY WERE ALL KNEELING DOWN!

"Silent Night"